CIRCLE JILL

AN EROTIC ADVENTURE

VICTORIA RUSH

VOLUME 40

JADE'S EROTIC ADVENTURES - BOOK 40

COPYRIGHT

For the uninhibited...

WANT TO AMP UP YOUR SEX LIFE?

Sign up for my newsletter to receive more free books and other steamy stuff. Discover a hundred different ways to wet your whistle!

Victoria Rush Erotica

1

———

"Hi Han," I said, kissing my best friend and registered sex therapist, Hannah, on the cheek.

"Hey beautiful," she said, giving me a big hug. "How was your business trip?"

"Eventful," I said, taking a window seat at our favorite restaurant overlooking the Navy Pier.

We were meeting for our customary weekly downtown luncheon to get caught up, and I was eager to tell her about my latest adventure visiting Washington, DC.

"Never a dull moment with you, girl," she said, ordering a margarita when the waiter came to our table.

"You have no idea," I said, nodding to the waiter to double the order. "I almost got arrested this time."

"What?!" she said, almost spilling her water after taking a quick sip.

"Yeah, for *turning tricks*, no less."

"You *what*?" she said, coughing as her water went down the wrong way. "What the hell were you doing that for? It's not like you're suffering for sex these days. Or for money, for that matter."

"I kind of fell into it. A guy I picked up in a bar left me some money when we finished our business, thinking I was a hooker."

"Why did he think that?"

"Well, I was tarted up pretty good and maybe a little easier to get in the sack than usual..."

"How did that lead to your almost getting *arrested*?"

"After that first night, I started to wonder how much I could make if I really set my mind to it. So for the remainder of my stay, I decided to make a concerted effort to pick up new customers each night...."

"How much are we *talking* here?" Hannah said, pinching her eyebrows. "I thought the going rate was like fifty bucks for a blowjob and maybe a hundred for some quick intercourse."

"Not in one of the most expensive hotels in DC, it isn't. I ended up pulling in more than three G's for three nights' work."

"Holy shit!" Hannah said, taking a gulp of her margarita after the waiter returned with our drinks. "I'd almost give up my *counseling* job for that kind of money!"

"That's what I was thinking. It's highly addictive get paid to have sex. But I suppose I was pressing my luck going back to the same upscale bar every night. I think I was being watched by an undercover cop."

"Did he have his way with you before he put the cuffs on you?"

"*She.* And yes she did. But there were no cuffs involved. I think she realized I was a new to this sort of thing and decided to give me a warning. But not before we fucked each other silly with a big pink dildo for the better part of two hours."

"You and your crazy escapades," Hannah said, shaking

her head. "One of these days they're going to be your undoing."

"Maybe," I smiled. "But at least I'll die happy."

"How's everything going otherwise?"

"Pretty good. But I had a sex-related question I wanted to ask you today."

"About how not to get arrested while playing out your wildest fantasies?"

"No," I laughed. "It's about my increasing propensity to squirt and emit fluid when I have sex..."

"A lot of women would be *happy* to have your problem," Hannah chuckled, peering over the top of her glass as she licked the salty rim.

"That's kind of what I wanted to ask you about. Am I just a weirdo? Why do I seem to be the only one among my long list of female lovers who can do this?"

"Actually," Hannah said, placing her glass back down on the table. "*Every* woman has the ability to squirt when she comes. Most of the fluid comes from a special gland surrounding the urethra called the Skene's gland. It's somewhat equivalent to the male prostate gland insofar as it empties into the urethra if sufficiently stimulated and ejects through your pee hole. But most women have trained their pubococcygeus muscles to resist the flow because it feels like you're peeing when you release the fluid."

"So it's *not* actually pee?"

"No, it's a clear, mostly tasteless fluid. It actually helps with the reproductive function by providing useful nutrients for sperm to make their way up a woman's reproductive tract after a man ejaculates. If you go back far enough into the history of far Eastern cultures, there's a fairly robust record of women ejaculating when they had sex. It's only a recent phenomenon of our somewhat repressed Christian culture where women have been trained to withhold this natural phenomenon."

"Wow," I said, taking a healthy swig of my margarita. "I had no idea. How come I'm the only one who seems to have learned to unleash the beast, in a manner of speaking?"

"You have to be extraordinarily relaxed and at ease with your partner to feel comfortable coming all over them. Maybe it's because you mostly have sex with *women* now and there's no competitive pressure to see who can outsquirt who. Or maybe it's because you've had so many partners and you've learned how to release your waters."

"Hmm," I said, nodding as I began to feel my pulse return to normal. "So I'm not a deviant, then?"

"Far from it. You could almost argue that the women who *resist* their natural ability to ejaculate are the abnormal ones. I actually have a friend who conducts workshops teaching women how to do this."

"What, in *person*? Live and in the *buff*?"

"There's no other way. It gets pretty explicit actually. Part of the process is revealing exactly where your G-spot is and how to properly stimulate it."

"So, there's a bunch of women in these workshops spreading their pussies for one another to see while jilling themselves in full view of the other participants?"

"Exactly," Hannah said. "You might want to try it some-time. Besides being incredibly arousing, you might be able to teach some of the other girls a thing or two from your own successful experience."

"That's crazy," I said, suddenly intrigued about this masturbation seminar. "What's the name of your friend's workshop and how do I find her?"

"You can find her online. Search for Laila's Fountain of Venus Workshop."

"*Fountain of Venus*," I smiled. "What a lovely name for something I'd always found kind of dirty and embarrassing."

"Far from it. I think you'll find the experience quite liberating. It's all about reclaiming your natural female birthright and learning to express your sexuality fully."

W hen I got home, I flipped open my laptop and plugged in the search words, eager to learn more about this fascinating workshop. When the website came up, it was tastefully designed with beautiful pictures of Georgia O'Keefe erotic flowers and soft, romantic music. The homepage described how the workshop was transformative, helping women overcome negative body images and repressive attitudes to heal their bodies and learn to realize their full sexual potential.

As I clicked on the various links in the menu bar about 'Body Image', 'How to Orgasm', 'Understanding your G-Spot, and 'Freeing your Lotus Spring', I became more and more excited about attending one of the sessions. Although I didn't need help learning how to squirt myself, the idea of watching ten other women rubbing their pussies together and seeing them squirt in unison was incredibly exciting. The price wasn't cheap at one thousand dollars, but that included three full days including all meals and accommodation at a four-star hotel.

I clicked on the Schedule tab and frowned when I saw that the next four sessions were already booked. I'd have to wait more than a month to get in on the next available one in New York City. After entering my credit card information and contact details, I sat back in my chair, feeling my heart pumping excitedly in my chest. It would require another trip away from home, but this time *I'd* be the one paying to have sex, and it would be in a secure environment along with ten other consenting adults. I noticed a wet stain spreading in the crotch of my jeans and pulled off my clothes and spread my thighs, staring at my dripping vulva.

"Maybe you're not such a weirdo after all," I said, talking to my pussy as I placed two fingers inside my opening and began rubbing my swollen G-Spot. As I closed my eyes and imagined watching the other women rubbing their pussies while they watched me, I could already feel the familiar pangs of an oncoming ejaculation building up inside me.

2

On the day of my scheduled workshop, I packed excitedly and left early for my flight to La Guardia. The website had recommended I pack a comfortable robe, plenty of thick bath towels, lots of lube, a large makeup mirror, a flashlight, and my favorite sex toy. By the time I closed the suitcase, there was barely enough room for my regular clothes.

Shouldn't be a problem, I thought. *It's not like we're going to need any with a bunch of nude women sitting around a circle showing off their pussies all day.*

The workshop started at 1 p.m. the first day, so I checked into my hotel after I landed and threw some essentials into a tote bag then headed uptown to the address provided for the instructor's West Side co-op. When Laila greeted me at the door, I noticed a ring of reclining chairs arranged in a circle in the middle of her large living room overlooking Central Park. Her apartment was tastefully decorated with symbols of erotic art and sculpture, including a large Shunga painting of a naked Japanese woman appearing to pee into an urn while she massaged her vulva.

Some of the women had already arrived, and we awkwardly introduced ourselves while we sampled hors d'oeuvres laid out on a buffet table while soft instrumental music played in the background and a flowery incense permeated the room. Most of the participants had already changed into their robes, and as we chatted amongst ourselves, Laila circulated making small talk, trying to ease the nervous tension in the room. She was older than I expected, maybe in her early fifties, but beautiful with long gray hair, bright blue eyes, and a curvy Madonna-like figure that I couldn't help stealing glances at whenever her back was turned. When the last attendee arrived and we'd all changed into our robes, she asked us to take a seat in one of the lounges and make ourselves comfortable.

The lounge chairs were shaped in a flattened S-curve with a tight webbing of Gore-tex fabric to prevent staining and facilitate easy cleaning. The back and leg rests were sloped at the ideal angle to recline comfortably while still being able to view our own bodies and those of our seat-mates easily. The whole atmosphere had an upscale hippie vibe to it, and I nodded at Laila's preparation, who obviously had conducted these workshops many times before.

"Thank you all for coming," she said, lying in the last empty lounge chair as some of the women chuckled at her unintended pun.

As I peered around the circle, I noticed the group included a wide range of ages, from a cute redhead looking to be somewhere in her early twenties to an attractive older woman in her late sixties. But most of them looked to be in their thirties and forties, with varying body shapes from slender and sylphlike to plump and rotund. While we all lay comfortably on our lounge chairs wearing nothing but body-hugging robes, I could feel the sexual tension in the room as the scent of feminine perfume mingled with the smoky incense.

"Feel free to help yourself to refreshments at any time," Laila said. "And if you haven't found them yet, there are two restrooms at the end of the corridor in the direction of the bedrooms. Is everybody feeling comfortable?"

"Mmm-hmm," the women murmured, nodding their heads enthusiastically.

"On this first afternoon of our three-day workshop, we're going to take things slow to start. Since this is all about overcoming the barriers to expressing our full feminine potential, I thought we'd begin with some introductions. If you feel comfortable, please share with us your purpose for attending, what you're hoping to gain from this workshop, and what impediments you've experienced in your journey of sexual exploration. And please don't be shy about sharing any of your feelings. This a safe environment where we're all here to support one another and learn from each other's experience. Am I right, ladies?"

"Absolutely," a pretty brunette in her thirties enthused.

"Okay then," Laila said. "Who'd like to start?"

A woman looking to be in her late forties raised her hand slowly and Laila nodded toward her.

"Yes, what is your name?"

"My name's Ava," the woman said. "I was hesitant about coming to this workshop, but a friend recommended it to me. My issue is that I've never been able to orgasm with a partner. My husband and I have been married for over twenty years, but during that time I've never come while having sex. I don't know if it's a mental block or if there's something wrong with me..."

"Thank you for sharing, Ava," Laila said. "First, I want you to know that there is nothing wrong with you and that this is a fairly common concern. The reasons for your inability to climax can have many sources. May I ask if you can orgasm through self-stimulation?"

"Yes..." the woman answered tentatively.

"That's a good sign," Laila nodded. "The reason for a woman's inability to orgasm with her partner is often grounded in expectations set by their family, or sometimes simply from the inexperience of your partner. Good open, honest communication between both partners is essential, but it starts with the understanding that it is normal, healthy, and perfectly natural for both partners to enjoy the sexual union together. We will address many of these issues in our workshop, and I'm confident you'll be able to elevate your sexual experience with your husband so that both of you enjoy your connection equally."

"Thank you," Ava said, unfolding her clamped arms over her chest and resting her hands in her lap.

"Who'd like to go next?" Laila said, peering around the circle.

The pretty brunette who'd interjected earlier raised her hand and Laila nodded toward her.

"My name's Claire," she said. "My reason for coming to the workshop is that I've been finding myself increasingly attracted to women, but I've been uncomfortable approaching them physically after so many years of failed heterosexual relationships. I thought by attending this seminar and seeing other women naked in a safe environment, it might help me break down the walls in a manner of speaking."

"Well, you've come to the right place, Claire," Laila said. "This is indeed a safe, nonjudgmental environment where all of us will be looking to become more comfortable in the presence of other women in a sexual context. I suspect others attending today share your motivation and that this forum will provide an uplifting introduction to the pleasures of same-sex discourse."

An African-American woman with a short afro raised her hand, and Laila nodded toward her.

"My name's Trinity, and I just wanted to tell Claire that as a proud lesbian since separating from my husband ten years ago, there's a whole new world of pleasure out there for you once you find a suitable partner. My purpose for attending the workshop is to learn new techniques for stimulating and arousing my partner. I find everybody's built differently and has different turn-ons, and I'm always looking for new ways to excite my lover."

"Indeed there is," Laila said. "And that's very well said, Trinity. Part of the purpose of this workshop from *my* perspective is to show that we all come in different shapes, sizes, and configurations, and that there is no one 'right' profile for becoming sexually actualized and learning to truly accept who we are."

Suddenly, a bunch of hands around the circle began to rise as the other women grew increasingly eager to share their goals and stories.

"Yes," Laila said, nodding toward a cute redhead in her mid-twenties.

"My name's Piper," she said. "My reason for coming to the workshop is that I've never been able to orgasm at *all*, from self-stimulation or partner sex. I don't know if you can help me, but I just want to learn what it actually feels like to come any way I can."

"Thank you for sharing, Piper," Laila nodded. "This is a more common phenomenon than many women realize. I want to assure you that you're not alone, and that learning to orgasm can be a transformative experience. We will be taking our time at first to explore our bodies in order to become fully comfortable and relaxed. Every woman has the ability to orgasm, and once you learn how, there's never any going back!"

The rest of the women in the room chuckled as more hands flew up in the air.

"Yes," Laila said, nodding toward a pretty Hispanic woman in her early forties.

"My name's Carla, and I'm not going to lie. My main reason for coming to this workshop is to learn how to squirt! No matter how much I try or how many online videos I watch, I can never seem to make it happen. Your website mentioned this was something we were going to explore, and I'm eager to see if you can help me."

"Yes, Carla," Laila chuckled. "That's one of the things we will explore towards the second half of our workshop. You may actually be surprised to know that *every* woman is equipped with the tools and anatomy to ejaculate. Much like other forms of sexual expression, it begins with accepting this is a normal and healthy part of your sexual experience and learning the proper technique to turn on your Lotus Spring.

"Who'd like to go next?"

A hot-looking blonde in her forties suddenly interjected.

"While we're on the subject of female ejaculation, I'd like to share my goal of learning how to make my *lover* squirt. My name's Hailey, and I've never really had a problem with ejaculating myself, but no matter how hard I try, I just can't seem to produce the same fireworks with my girlfriend. She's actually become somewhat self-conscious about it and I was hoping to bring back some new techniques to help her turn the corner."

By the time all the women had finished introducing

themselves, everybody had become more relaxed, laughing and supporting one another while we shared our goals and sexual frustrations. When my turn came, I explained that I'd simply come with an open mind to learn some new techniques, not wanting to share that really I was just excited to watch a bunch of other hot women masturbating openly. Laila introduced herself last, explaining that she'd been a sex therapist and counsellor for many years, but that she'd found these live workshops were the best way to help women overcome their sexual blocks and become fully actualized.

After a short refreshment break, she lit some candles to set the mood for the next stage in our journey of erotic self-exploration.

"Now that we've gotten to know one another a little better and shared our goals, the next step is to bare *another* piece of ourselves by disrobing. The purpose of this step is to learn more about our own bodies and to appreciate that every woman is built differently. The first step in realizing our full potential is recognizing the inner and outer beauty that we all share regardless of our skin color, body type, or sexual persuasion. To that end, whenever you feel comfortable, I'd like you to remove your robe and lay down on your chaise chair completely naked. You may wish to place some towels underneath you, as inevitably there will be some bodily fluids involved."

As everyone slowly removed their robes and placed them in their bags beside them on the floor, it became more apparent that each of the women had a different body shape and size. Some of the women were rotund with rolls around their bellies and large pendulous breasts, some were slender with barely perceptible tits, and others were curvy and voluptuous with sexy hips and proud bouncing boobs.

Some of them lay confidently on their reclining chairs with their bodies fully exposed and their legs slightly parted revealing the dark slit in their pussies, while others lay more demurely with their legs pressed tightly together and their arms crossed over their chest trying to protect their modesty. I peered over at Laila, who'd joined the rest of the group lying buck naked, and I felt my pussy moistening while I soaked up her curvy, well-toned body.

"Right then," she smiled with a twinkle in her eye. "That wasn't so difficult, was it?"

Everybody laughed nervously while squirming in their chairs.

"The first thing I want you to do is peer around the circle and notice how each of us is built differently. There is no one standard size or shape for a woman, and we should revel in the uniqueness that defines each of us while at the same time admiring the wonderful disparity in the female form. Isn't it marvelous to see the exciting differences between us and realize that, like a snowflake or an individual flower, there are no two that are alike?"

Each of us peered around the circled and nodded in appreciation at the smorgasbord of feminine beauty laid out before us.

"Like good food, it's the *variety* that makes our experience as women truly interesting and satisfying. Can you imagine always eating chocolate cake for dessert or having waffles with maple syrup for breakfast every day? As lovely and appetizing as these dishes may be, we would soon tire of them and they'd lose their allure if that was all we ever had to experience. I want you to take a moment to bask in the innate beauty of each of your colleagues and soak up their unique body styles so that we can fully appreciate the inherent beauty within each of us. Let's give a round of applause to recognize the unique beauty that all of us share."

While Laila began to clap softly, the group slowly joined in, until thunderous applause filled the room as we all peered around the circle beaming at one another with broad smiles.

"Yes, indeed," Laila said, nodding approvingly. "We are all beautiful and unique in our own special way. But one thing we all have in *common* is that we are all proud owners of that wonderful part of our anatomy called our vulvas. The fount of life itself, this amazing organ is capable of giving us incredible pleasure, unifying us with our partners, and bringing new life into this world. And just as with the *other* parts of our bodies, each woman's vulva is shaped and configured differently.

"If you feel comfortable, I'd like you to begin spreading your legs apart to reveal your sacred temple and notice how each of our vulvas have a different shape, color, and configuration. Just as with the rest of our body, there is no one perfect pussy. Like a blossoming flower, our folds and contours are shaped differently, and it is our multiplicity that makes each of us special and interesting. Raise your knees up and take a long moment to peer at your beautiful pussy, touching and stretching your folds to examine it carefully. Celebrate your womanhood and accept that you are the best possible *you* you can be. Proudly show your colleagues around the circle your exquisite yoni and don't be ashamed of your unique configuration. Every one of us is different, and every one of us is beautiful!"

As we all peered around the room staring at each other's pussies, I was fascinated by the incredible diversity of colors, shapes, and sizes. I'd been with a lot of women in my life, but somehow seeing the ten of us fully exposed with our cunnies framed by our spread legs on the low-lying lounges truly revealed the wide range of morphology that we all shared. Some of the women's pussies had dark brown labia while others had pink or pale white lips. Some of the lips were full and puffy, and some were thin and tight. Some hung in convoluted folds like a piece of drapery resting on the floor, whereas others were strung as tight as a freshly tuned lute.

Some women had hairy bushes, some had neatly trimmed pubic mounds, and some, like me, were totally bald. In some of the women's vulvas I could clearly see their clitoris standing tall and proud, a pink bulb poking out from its protective hood like a little piggy in a blanket, whereas in other women it was neatly concealed under the fold of skin at the top of their slits. It was strangely *non-erotic* taking it all in, and I was utterly mesmerized by the spectacle of it all.

"This is one of my favorite moments," Laila said, smiling broadly as she watched each of the women appraising each other's vulvas and nodding approvingly. "When we can revel in the common beauty that defines us as women and embrace the differences that make each of us unique. Now, I want you to take a closer look at your beautiful yonis by taking out the mirrors I asked each of you to bring with you, as well as your flashlights. If it's a lighted makeup mirror that you brought, plug it into the extension cord resting beside each of your lounges. If not, point your flashlight so that it shines directly on your vulva and position your mirror so you can see your flower from the perspective of an imaginary lover."

It took each of us a few minutes to get everything set up properly and to position our bodies and mirrors to see our pussies close up, but when we did, I heard some audible gasps and deep breathing coming from my seatmates. For many of the women, it was obvious this was the first time they'd looked at their pussies this close-up.

"Take a moment this time to truly examine every part of your magnificent vulva," Laila said. "Spread your lips apart and examine the space between your labia. Notice the size and shape of your clitoral bulb and hood, find the position of your urethral opening between your clit and your vagina, and pinch your thick outer labia and thinner inner labia. Slide your fingers all the way down your pudendum and along the edges of your labia as you bask in the sights and sensations of this most amazing part of a woman's anatomy. Squeeze your pelvic muscles and notice how your skin flexes all the way from the top of your vulva to your anus. Watch how your pussy moistens as you touch it and spread it apart, like a beautiful flower blossoming with dew in the springtime. You are truly one of a kind and incredibly beautiful in every way."

I'd spent enough time peering at my own and other woman's pussies over the past few years, but I'd never really taken the time to clinically analyze the shape and configuration of my cunny, nor those of other women for that matter. As I stared at my tiny pee hole while I stretched and squeezed my lips, watching it flex open and shut, I shook my head marveling at all the parts I'd never paid attention to, amazed at the complexity and unifying beauty of my female instrument.

After a few minutes, I looked up and noticed all the other women staring at their pussies with equal wonderment and awe, every one of them with huge smiles on their faces while they reveled in their unique beauty. Even though none of us had so much as *tried* to stimulate ourselves sexually, it was one of the most exciting and uplifting experiences I'd ever experienced in the company of other women.

When Laila ended the session about thirty minutes later, inviting all of us to her favorite restaurant later that evening, I noticed a certain glow and contented smile in the women as we said our temporary goodbyes upon leaving her apartment. I had no idea what was in store for the rest of our three-day workshop, but I'd already gained a new appreciation for my sexual instrument as well as that of my female partners, and I found myself walking with a happy lilt as I flagged a cab to head back to my hotel.

3

We all enjoyed a delicious sushi dinner later that evening, laughing and learning much more about each of our histories, predilections, and erotic desires. By the time we all headed back to our hotels around 10 p.m., everybody was far more relaxed and comfortable about sharing our sexual experiences. That night, I had a strange dream where I was shrunken to the size of a dildo while I buzzed in front of Laila's vulva as she masturbated herself to orgasm. I had no idea what the meaning of the dream was, but I certainly woke up eager to see more of our attractive workshop leader's pussy close-up.

The following morning, we all showed up at her apartment at 9 a.m. and quickly disrobed, assuming our usual positions on the reclining lounges. I noticed this time that all of the women were more comfortable about revealing their pussies, spreading their legs wide apart as they proudly showed off their erotic flowers.

"I hope everybody had a restful night," Laila said, lying naked on her lounge two positions to my left. "Today we're going to explore our beautiful vulvas more closely and learn more about what goes on *inside* our vaginas, especially with regard to the mysterious G-Spot. As we will see, the G-Spot holds many wonderful surprises, including the magical wellspring of waters that allows us to express our full feminine potential.

"But first, we're going to baseline our erotic experience by masturbating in our familiar manner. This is where you're welcome to use the vibrators that you brought with you, or if you prefer, simply use your hand to stimulate yourself. As with yesterday, I don't want anybody to feel self-conscious in any way. We're all here to support one another and enjoy the shared experience. So without any further ado, feel free to spread your legs and enjoy yourselves."

We all looked at one another for a moment, then each of us reached into our tote bags, removing our favorite vibrators. I recognized many familiar toys that I'd used myself, including the popular Rabbit, Magic Wand, and Pocket Rocket. But when I pulled out my Osé vibrator, the women peered at me with a curious look on their faces, having never seen the strange-looking device. Formed in the shape of a hand, the 'palm' had a large opening where a tongue-like appendage flapped against my clit, and a long, curved finger which flexed inside me to stimulate my G-Spot.

While everybody checked their batteries and plugged in their devices, I noticed Laila slipping the C-shaped We-Vibe device into her slit, pulling it tightly against her vulva as the other women began caressing their pussies. As the whirring and humming noises began to fill the room, I could hear soft moans emanating around the circle as the women began to spread their legs further apart and rolled their hips in escalating pleasure.

I slipped the finger of the Osé vibrator inside me and tapped the remote-control device to activate the undulating tongue action and groaned at the familiar feeling of the slippery appendage lapping against my flaring clit. I'd used the device many times before, but watching ten other women playing with their pussies at the same time raised my pleasure tenfold. I was mesmerized peering around the circle, seeing how each woman used their devices and watching the rising look of ecstasy on their faces.

Ava, the woman who couldn't come with her husband, held her magic wand tightly between her legs with two hands, tilting her hips upwards as she pressed the industrial-strength vibrator hard against her clit.

No wonder she couldn't climax with her husband, I thought. If that's the way she's become accustomed to orgasming, who could possibly compete with that?

Claire, the woman around my age who'd confessed to being newly attracted to women, used a plain pink vibrating dildo, sliding it slowly between her lips while she stared wide-eyed at the other women rubbing their pussies beside her. Carla, the attractive Hispanic woman who said she wanted to learn how to squirt, used the small but powerful Pocket Rocket vibrator to focus all of the unit's power directly on her clit as her mouth gaped open in pleasure.

Trinity, the pretty African-American lesbian who said she wanted to learn new techniques for stimulating her partner, inserted her big Rabbit vibrator deep into her hole while she pulled her legs together and rammed the dildo in and out of her cunt. Piper, the cute redhead who said she'd never been able to orgasm at all, used her right hand to massage her vulva while she stared at the strange collection of electronic devices the other women were using to stimulate themselves.

I peered over at Laila and noticed that she was resting fairly still on her lounge chair as she quietly pressed the base of her vibrator harder against her pussy. She seemed to be watching the other women intently, like she was *studying* their technique rather than losing herself in her own pleasure as her vibrator hummed silently inside her.

But as the moans and groans of the other women began to grow more prominent, I felt my own pleasure beginning to rise, and I switched on the flexing finger action of the Osé vibrator, feeling it rubbing against the base of my G-Spot. It was obvious that many of the women were nearing their climaxes as their bodies began to tense and their grip on their vibrators grew tighter.

Trinity was the first to pop off as she grabbed the base of her Rabbit vibrator and pulled it hard against her vulva with two hands, shaking vigorously as her whole body jerked and spasmed on the reclining chair. Soon after, Ava came, as a deep rash spread over her chest and her mouth gaped open in the throes of climax while she held her big vibrator hard against her dripping pussy.

Overcome by the sight of the other women coming, Claire couldn't hold back any longer as she thrust her skinny dildo deep into her snatch and flapped her thighs in and out, moaning loudly along with the others. Carla was the next one to lose control, as she lifted her hips high off the base of her chair, pressing the chrome nubs of her Pocket Rocket hard against her clit while her pelvic floor muscles pulsed in a series of powerful contractions.

By now, Piper was rubbing her vulva furiously with her hand, trying desperately to get off with the other women, but as her whole body flushed near the tipping point, she suddenly stopped, breathing heavily in her chair with a disappointed look on her face.

The last one to come before I did was Hailey, the hot blonde in her forties who'd said she didn't have any trouble squirting, but that she'd come to the workshop to learn how to make her partner ejaculate. Her technique was a little different from most of the other girls, employing both of her hands to stimulate her pussy instead of a vibrator. As her right hand circled her engorged clitoris, she curled two fingers of her other hand inside her pussy, rubbing the entrance of her hole rapidly while she clenched her buttocks and slowly lifted her ass off the surface of her chair. As her moans grew progressively louder, she let out a loud yelp and pulled her fingers out of her cunt, squirting high up into the air in a series of powerful gushes.

I peered over at Laila who was nodding as she watched Hailey coming, then she turned toward me just as I began to feel my own body tightening on the brink of climax. As I spread my legs wide apart and began to jet my fluids out the side of my pussy onto my quivering thighs, she pressed her curved vibrator harder against her pussy, jerking softly in her chair while we shared a long, simultaneous orgasm.

When all of the grunting and moaning finally stopped, the women peered around the circle and began to laugh. This was probably the first time any of us had done something this audacious, and after seeing how much fun it was witnessing other women releasing their sexual inhibitions together, all we could do was laugh at how wonderfully liberating it felt.

4

———

After we all cleaned up and replaced the wet towels underneath us, Laila pulled the We-Vibe vibrator out of her pussy and placed it on the floor beside her chair.

"Well that certainly looked like fun," she smiled. "What do you think, girls, did you enjoy that?"

"Oh yeah," Hailey said, still patting down the insides of her wet thighs and ass.

"Definitely," Trinity said.

"Oh my God," Claire enthused. "That was the hottest thing I've ever experienced!"

"Did you find this to be a relaxed introduction to having sex with other women?" Laila smiled.

"I'm not sure *relaxed* is the right word," she said, still trying to collect her breath. "It looks like I've got a long way to go to catch up with everybody when it comes to using the latest toys."

"Vibrators can be a fun addition to your sex life," Laila nodded. "There's certainly an abundance of different shapes and designs to satisfy anyone's curiosity. But sometimes the greatest pleasure can be had by using our fingers and other parts of our bodies to stimulate ourselves and our lovers."

Laila peered over in Piper's direction and smiled.

"How about you, Piper? How did you find the experience?"

"It was incredibly arousing watching all the other women stimulating themselves and coming so powerfully. I could feel my body tingling all over, but I still don't think I came."

"You'd certainly know if you did," Laila said. "But don't worry. Learning to orgasm takes longer for some women than others. As we saw yesterday, everybody is different, and every woman has a different sexual history. The key is learning how to relax and enjoying the *journey* rather than focusing entirely on the destination. When you're ready, it will definitely come."

"I hope so," she said. "Because judging by the expressions of the other women around the room, I'm definitely ready for some of that."

As the rest of the group chuckled, Laila reached down beside her, placing an unusual object on her lap.

"I noticed while I was watching each of you that most of you concentrated on stimulating the *external* part of your vulva. But did you know that the clitoris is actually much larger and goes much deeper than you might believe?"

She held the plastic object up in the air and turned it slowly for each of us to see. Looking a bit like an oversize praying mantis, it had a long pointed 'nose' and large flappy wings extending out from its body.

"This is a scale model of an actual clitoris, showing both the *external* parts we're all familiar with, and the *internal* parts that comprise the bulk of the structure."

She slid her finger along the protruding proboscis, caressing her way down over the flaring wings of the model.

"Like the tip of an iceberg, the clitoral glans and shaft that we see on the outside of our vulva only represents a tiny fraction of this magnificent organ. The rest of your clitoris rests *inside* your vagina, spreading out and surrounding the walls of your tunnel with sensitive, erectile tissue that provides its own kind of unique pleasure when properly stimulated. So, in a way, there's no such thing as a clitoral vs. vaginal orgasm—they're actually the same thing. Whether you orgasm from internal or external stimulation or a combination of the two, different parts of your clitoris are being stimulated either way."

"Why can't I come with my husband when we have intercourse then?" Ava said, crossing her arms in frustration.

"The glans of our clitoris, which is what we're most familiar with on the outside of our vulva, has the most concentrated nerve endings and it can be easy for some of us to focus our attention there, since it's often the easiest and surest way to get off. But if we become too acclimated to reaching orgasm purely from external stimulation, sometimes it can be difficult to train ourselves to enjoy the process of penetration with our partners. But there's *another* organ inside our vaginas that has the power to take our pleasure to a whole new level. And that is our *G-Spot*. How many of you have heard of the G-Spot?"

Virtually every woman around the circle raised their hands without hesitation.

"How many of you know where it is?"

Most of the women raised their hands, but more tentatively this time.

"Would anybody like to explain?"

Trinity raised her hand and Laila nodded for her to speak.

"It's on the inside of our vaginas on the upper wall, close to our pubic bone."

"That's true," Laila said. "Do you exactly how *far* inside?"

"I'm not a hundred percent sure," Trinity said. "Towards the back?"

"Actually, the G-Spot, like the clitoris, is quite a bit larger and shaped differently than many of us have been led to believe. It's an egg-shaped bump that starts about two inches inside our vagina and tapers toward the back of the cavity. We can actually see it with the right equipment and technique. How many of you would like to see your G-Spots for the first time?"

"Yes, please!" Carla interjected excitedly.

"Okay," Laila said. "Take out your flashlights and mirrors once again and position them in front of your vulvas like we did yesterday."

Laila waited a few minutes until everybody was properly set up, then she moved her own mirror to the side so everyone could see her pussy clearly from around the circle.

"Follow along with me as I show you the simple steps for revealing this amazing organ."

Laila placed the index finger of each hand gently inside her hole then slowly pulled her lips apart.

"Place a finger from each hand inside your vagina and slowly spread it apart until you can clearly see your vaginal opening. Now, push your pelvic floor muscles forward like you're bearing down to deliver a baby. You'll see the tissue inside your vagina begin to press out. Continue until you see a little bump on the top of your vagina with horizontal ridges running across its surface..."

As Laila demonstrated the technique, our eyes all

bulged out when we saw the protruding bump clearly high-lighted by her flashlight.

"That little swelling with the horizontal ridges is your G-Spot," she said. "Isn't it magnificent? Now you try it."

The room became so silent you could hear a pin drop as the rest of the women followed Laila's instructions, peering intently into their propped-up mirrors while they stretched their labia apart. Suddenly, one woman after another gasped when she saw her G-Spot up close and personal for the first time. As I gaped at my own in wonderment, I could hardly believe that I'd never actually *seen* it after so much experimenting with sex with other men and women.

"It's pretty incredible, isn't it?" Laila said, smiling broadly as she panned around the room peering at all the women staring at their pussies with wide eyes.

"Now insert the two middle fingers of your primary hand into your opening and feel the shape and size of your G-Spot."

She demonstrated the technique for everyone else to see as she sunk the two middle fingers of her right hand into her pussy, pressing her two outer fingers up against the side of her thighs.

"Run your two fingers along the trough on the side of the bulge, squeezing it gently between your fingers. Can you feel how it's spongy, almost like a water-filled balloon?"

Many of the women nodded as they turned their hands slowly with their fingers embedded inside their pussies.

"Feel the ridges on the leading edge of your G-Spot, where it's most prominent. Notice that it's only one-and-a-half to two inches inside your vagina. Now, still squeezing it gently between your two fingers, press your fingers deeper inside your pussy, noticing how the bulge tapers off toward some soft, fluffy tissue about four inches inside."

Laila reached down beside her then passed a picture around the circle showing an object that looked like the cotton-candy sticks at the fair.

"Unknown to many women," she continued. "This bulge inside the front of your vaginas is actually a separate *organ* called the Skene's gland. The Skene's gland is somewhat equivalent to a man's prostate, even sharing a similar chemical makeup containing an enzyme called prostate specific antigen, or PSA. The fluid inside this gland, which is what causes the bulge inside your vagina, produces a clear, colorless liquid that empties into your urethra and is emitted through your pee hole."

"Is this where a woman's *ejaculate* comes from?" Piper said, shaking her head in amazement.

"Primarily, yes," Laila nodded. "But because it feels like you're about to pee when it's expressed, most women have trained themselves to hold it in when they orgasm by contracting their pelvic floor muscles."

"So it's not actually *urine* even though it comes out the same hole?" Claire said.

"No," Laila said. "I'm going to teach your how to express this gland in a few minutes and you'll see that it has a completely different color, smell, and chemical composition than urine. In fact, scientists have recently discovered that the fluid emitted by this gland facilitates contraception by providing essential nutrients for sperm as they make their way up the reproductive tract after ejaculation."

"So, if a woman ejaculates at the same time as her husband, it actually *increases* the chances of conception?" Carla asked. "Why haven't we been taught about this in our sex education classes? The discussion always seems to focus on the *man's* role in inseminating the woman with his sperm!"

"I'm not entirely sure," Laila said, nodding her head sympathetically. "Maybe it's because until fairly recently women weren't encouraged to enjoy sex, let alone to the extent they could ejaculate in a manner similar to men. It may also be a product of our repressed Western culture. For thousands of years, other cultures have known about, encouraged, and even celebrated the natural ability of every woman to ejaculate. Many of them would spread the waters upon their bodies or even *drink* it, believing it had magical healing qualities."

"Is that what the woman in the illustration on the wall is doing?" Trinity asked, peering at the Japanese Shunga painting.

"Exactly. This painting created many centuries ago depicts a woman ejaculating into an urn while she's stimulating herself. Far from being embarrassed about the release of her female fluid while she's having sex, she doesn't want to waste a precious drop."

"Can you teach us how to do this too?" Trinity said.

"Absolutely," Laila said. "Now that you know exactly where your G-Spot is and how to manipulate it, it's actually quite easy. You can even do it without climaxing. Let's take it in baby steps. First let's learn how to express it, then we'll learn how to squirt when we orgasm, which you'll find takes your erotic experience to a whole new level of satisfaction."

Holy shit, I thought to myself. *Hannah wasn't kidding when she said this workshop would be enlightening.* I had no idea there was so much history and science behind the act of squirting, and I couldn't wait to try it out with my newfound friends.

                                5
                          ───────

Laila ordered sandwiches in for lunch, but it must
have been the shortest meal any of us had had in a
long time, we were all so excited to learn how to
use our newfound G-Spots. When we resumed our positions on our lounge chairs, all the women still had their
mirrors propped up expectantly between their legs. But
Laila told us to put them away, since the next exercise would
be guided mostly by feel. As I peered around the circle at
everyone's naked body, I was happy to have an unobstructed
view to watch the impending waterworks.

"Right, then," Laila said, taking her seat. "Your first order
of business is to place extra towels underneath you, perhaps
even doubling them under your butt. You'll be surprised
how much fluid this gland can eject, up to five times as
much as a man ejaculates when he comes."

Far from being irritated at Laila's frequent comparisons
to men, I appreciated how it made us feel empowered about
our own sexuality and that we should no longer feel like we
were taking a back seat to their enjoyment.

"But I also don't want you to feel any reluctance to let

your feminine waters flow," Laila said. "Both the hardwood floors and the vinyl-covered chairs can be easily cleaned. The first step in learning to ejaculate is removing any mental barriers to letting it all hang out, figuratively speaking."

Everyone giggled while we nodded excitedly.

"The one thing you'll need to get started is a little bit of lube. Although you'll be producing plenty of moisture by the time we finish, you'll want to make it easy to insert your fingers and massage your G-Spots with a minimum of friction. So place a healthy dollop on your two middle fingers while you lift your knees to a ninety-degree angle."

While everyone assumed the position, the women suddenly fell silent, as an electric charge filled the room.

"Before we actually begin massaging our G-Spots, first I want to conduct a little test. We're going to check the strength and elasticity of your perineal muscles."

Laila cupped her hands together with a small space between her palms.

"These are a pair of hammock-shaped muscles that run all the way from your pubic bone at the top of your vulva to your coccyx near your anus. Their primary role is to support your pelvic organs, but they also play a critical role in a woman's sexual and reproductive health. If they're too *tight*, this can cause pain in your pelvic region, and if they are too *loose*, this can contribute to incontinence."

"Is that why I frequently have pain in my lower abdomen when I have sex with my husband?" Claire asked.

"Possibly," Laila nodded. "Particularly if his penis is larger than most men's, or he's rough when you have sex. This can cause painful bruising of the cervix, which many women instinctively try to resist by clamping down on their PC muscles in an effort to control their partner's penetration. Over time, this chronic contraction of the perineal muscles causes cramping and other types of referred pain."

"He *is* quite large," Claire said. "But how else can I counteract his tendency to thrust so deeply inside me?"

"As with all healthy sex between partners," Laila said. "It starts with good, open, honest communication. When you explain the consequences of his actions, any loving husband should be willing to adjust his technique to please his partner. There are plenty of other ways for him to enjoy the act of sex, but it starts with him resisting the temptation to penetrate you fully, at least until he ejaculates. Besides, I have a feeling when you show him your new powers to squirt during sex, this will more than make up for any other concessions he might have to make. Most men, and women for that matter, get quite turned on seeing their partner ejaculate."

Many of the women chuckled, reflecting on the many porn videos they and their husbands had undoubtedly watched with the women squirting all over their partners when they came.

"Okay, now press your two fingers into your vaginal opening up to the first joint," Laila said. "Then squeeze them gently with your PC muscles. You should be able to insert them fairly easily, with a snug, but not overly tight fit. If you have difficulty squeezing them, your PC muscles may be too weak, whereas if you have difficulty pressing them inside or they feel too tightly compressed, your PC muscles may be too tense."

"What do we do if they're too weak?" Molly, the sixty-year-old woman said.

"Like any muscle, they atrophy from lack of use and can be strengthened with proper exercises. Simply contracting them often and attempting to hold your finger or other objects in your vagina will help. There are also a variety of PC muscle aids like Ben-Wa balls and vaginal barbells that you can buy to facilitate the strengthening process. It's especially important the older we get to keep these muscles well maintained, to avoid urinary problems."

"Can you show me where to buy these aids?" Molly asked.

"I'll leave each of you with a summary of links to reference and purchase most of the items I discuss during this workshop. But for now, simply understand that this is something that can be fairly easily fixed and improved."

"I seem to have the *opposite* problem," Claire said, frowning as she flexed her arm muscles while pressing her fingers inside her vagina. "I can barely get my fingers inside. It almost feels like I have a tourniquet around them."

"This is usually more of a *mental* problem than a physical one," Laila nodded. "The first step is learning to relax your PC muscles, realizing that you are in a safe zone where nobody can hurt you. Close your eyes and breathe slowly and deeply, concentrating on relaxing all the muscles in your pelvic region. Can you feel the pressure beginning to ease up on your fingers?"

"Yes," Claire said.

"Okay, now that we know how to optimize our PC muscles' strength and flexibility, let's begin to *stimulate* our G-Spot to make it engorged and full of fluid. Insert your two fingers a little deeper, up to the second joint until you feel the horizontal ridges of your gland, then press gently on the bump, massaging it gently in small circles."

Everybody closed their eyes while their hands moved slowly inside their pussies.

"Relax while you concentrate on the pleasurable sensations you're feeling. After a few minutes, you may feel the familiar sensation of an approaching orgasm, and the roof of your vagina will begin to balloon near the far end. If so, I want you to slow down and concentrate on your breathing. This first time we're going to learn to ejaculate *without* orgasm, then we'll make it a little more exciting by adding an erotic element to it."

As Laila instructed each of us what to do, she closed her eyes while she moved her fingers inside her pussy. I watched her pretty face and her rising and falling breasts, feeling my G-Spot becoming increasingly swollen and more aroused.

"Can you feel your G-Spot becoming engorged?"

"Yes," Ava said as the other women nodded silently.

"As you continue to stimulate your G-Spot, you'll begin to feel the sensation of needing to urinate. This is a good thing. Don't worry, you will not actually *pee*. There is an entirely different set of muscles that control the release of urine. As the urge to pee continues to build up inside you, begin to push out with your PC muscles like you did yesterday when you first examined your G-Spot. Hold it for a few seconds, then stop pushing but continue stimulating your G-spot. This will help to build up your ejaculatory juices. Your G-Spot should feel quite hard and swollen now."

"Yes," Carla panted. "I can feel it. Should I let it go now?"

"When you feel like you can't hold it any longer, remove your fingers from your opening and bear down. Don't clamp your PC muscles to *tighten* them, push to *release* like you're delivery a baby. As you begin to feel fluid coming out of your urethra, keep pushing. Remember, you are not peeing, you are *ejaculating* from your female prostrate. Release the spring and revel in your new feminine powers. Feel comfortable jetting your fluid all over your legs and your pussy while you ejaculate."

I turned in the direction of Laila and saw that her

buttocks were clamped tightly together while jets of clear fluid began pulsing out of her vulva in long and powerful streams.

"Oh!" Carla suddenly huffed, as her pussy began gushing a waterfall over her bare vulva and ass.

"Huh!" Claire exclaimed as she arched her back and jets began squirting from her elevated pussy.

"Oh my God!" Piper exclaimed as her pretty cunny began to express the clear fluid from her prostate.

One after another, every woman around the circle began to jet their ejaculate from their pussies, sighing and grunting in delight at their newfound ability to come on demand. Up to this point, I'd been holding mine in but when I saw all the others spraying all over their bodies and lounge chairs, I pulled my fingers out of my hole and proudly squirted my juices halfway across the room. For the first time in my life, I'd ejaculated without orgasm and it felt incredibly empowering, like I'd just discovered some kind of new superpower.

Talk about the Fountain of Venus, I smiled, watching the women tilting their hips so they could better watch the jets of liquid arcing out of their pussies. *That's the sexiest fountain I've ever seen.*

6

After all of the women had finished ejaculating, we all lay still on our lounges, not even bothering to clean up the mess we'd made spraying all over our bodies and the surrounding furniture. It was as if everybody wanted to revel in the feeling of their juices bathing their bodies, much like the afterglow after orgasm.

"Holy shit!" Ava said. "That was incredible. I've never been able to do that, and I didn't even climax!"

"Same here," Carlo said. "Finally–I can come like a *man*!"

Everybody laughed while we clapped our hands together, thrilled for ourselves and all the others that we'd been able to express this new dimension of our sexual powers.

"Yes," Laila nodded. "Isn't it liberating to know that we can express our full feminine powers whenever we want and no longer feel guilty about enjoying the sexual response to the fullest? For those of you in a *heterosexual* relationship, I think your partners will be surprised and delighted with your newfound ability to ejaculate. And for those of you in lesbian relationships, your partners will be *equally* excited and turned on with your shower of love."

"It felt wonderful," Piper nodded. "But I feel like I still haven't experienced a proper orgasm. When will we be able to experiment with this new technique and learn to *climax* at the same time?"

"I'm glad you asked, Piper," Laila said, passing around a box of tissues. "Because that will be the next step in our journey of self-exploration. First, why don't we all take a little break to collect our breath and clean up? But before we do, I'd like each of you to take a tissue and blot up some of the ejaculate you just emitted. Then if you really have to go pee, while you're in the restroom compare the smell and appearance of the two fluids. We'll discuss the results when we reconvene. If you thought that *last* exercise was liberating, wait until we add the sexual element to the equation. See you all again in fifteen minutes."

While we all cleaned up our seating arrangements and placed new towels down on our lounges, Laila put on some sexy music and replaced the incense burning in the room with a new, musky scent. When we all returned to our chairs, there was a new charge in the air as we peered at everyone's glistening bodies expectantly.

"Okay," Laila said, resuming her position in her chair. "What did you discover from your little pee-blotting comparison?"

"It's true what you said," Carla nodded, proudly holding up her two samples side by side. "The pee sample had a decidedly yellow tinge to it, whereas the female ejaculation blot was clear with no staining of the tissue at all."

"What about the *smell*?" Laila said. "Did you notice a difference there too?"

"Yes," Carla nodded. "The pee had a strong urine scent, while the ejaculate had almost no smell whatsoever."

"I think you'll find once you begin to introduce this new technique with your partners, that it *tastes* a lot more pleasant too," Laila smiled. "In fact, the large quantity of glucose in your prostatic fluid that provides nutrients for sperm is actually quite *sweet*. Yet another hidden benefit of our magical feminine spring."

"Mmm," Trinity purred, already beginning to imagine trying out this new technique with her lesbian lover.

"So, are you guys ready to take this to the next level?" Laila said with a big grin on her face. "Would you like to learn how to *orgasm* at the same time you ejaculate?"

"*Fuck* yes," Carla said.

"Yes please," Piper nodded.

As we all chuckled, Laila leaned over to pick up her We-Vibe sex toy, placing it beside her on her lounge chair.

"The first thing I want you to understand is that if you continue to rely purely on *external* clitoral stimulation to orgasm, you will usually be unable to ejaculate, at least in any noticeable quantity. You'll need to change your technique in order to squirt when you come, by stimulating your G-Spot in the same manner we just learned. But *this* time, we're going to imagine erotic scenes as we stimulate ourselves and try to produce a blended orgasm."

Laila picked up her vibrator and placed it back on the floor beside her.

"Although you're welcome to use sex toys to stimulate your clitoris, for our first attempt at orgasm with ejaculation, I'm going to recommend you use your fingers only. It's important that you concentrate on the sensations you experience *everywhere* around your vulva, including the opening of your urethra, which is at the tip of your G-Spot. To get started, you may wish to close your eyes as you try to relax and focus on your feelings without getting distracted by what your seatmates are doing, or feel the pressure to come at the same time or at the same pace they do.

"On the other hand, if watching your sisters massaging their vulvas and masturbating turns you on, feel free to watch and soak up the show. Shall we get started?"

"Absolutely!" Trinity said, eager to begin.

"As before, I want you to insert the two middle fingers of your dominant hand into your pussy and gently massage your G-Spot to build up the flow of fluid to your prostate and increase the pleasurable sensations around your internal clitoris. But this time, instead of trying to *resist* the urge to orgasm, feel free to stimulate your external clit with your other hand as you feel the pleasurable sensations building up within you. When you feel yourself ready to climax, bear down like you did before and let yourself enjoy the full experience of coming in the fullest sense of the word. Let's show all the men out there that they're not the only ones who can ejaculate when they come!"

As she inserted her fingers into her vagina and began to circle her clit with her other hand, the other women slid down on their lounges, spreading their legs wide apart while they followed her lead. Unlike the last time when everybody lay fairly still while they massaged their G-Spots, this time the women moaned and squirmed in their chairs as they began to enjoy the pleasurable sensations emanating from their bodies.

Although I was eager to come after our last exercise, I was content to watch all the other women enjoying themselves as they ramped up their arousal with their two-pronged stimulation of their vulvas. It seemed everyone had a different technique for stimulating their pussies. Some of the women massaged their entire vulvas in slow up and down techniques, where others diddled their clits with rapid flapping of their fingers directly over their button. But what unified us as a group was the sight of every one of us sinking the fingers of our *other* hand into our cunts while we squeezed and stimulated our rapidly enlarging G-Spots. I'd never really spent much time feeling how my G-Spot changed in size and shape when I masturbated, but this time I could feel it growing and swelling as the pleasure began to mount and spread throughout my body.

As I felt myself getting closer and closer to orgasm, I peered around the circle becoming increasingly turned on by the sight of the other women writhing and moaning as they neared their own sexual nirvana. I was particularly focused on Claire and Piper, knowing they were the two who had expressed the strongest desire to squirt and orgasm, and as I watched their bodies progressively tighten and flush, I could feel my own climax approaching like an unstoppable freight train.

When Carla began lifting her hips off her lounge and her whole body began to tense, I stared at her pussy, excited to see her squirt for the first time while simultaneously coming. Suddenly, she emitted a loud squeal and strong jets of clear fluid squirted out of her vulva in the direction of the other women in the circle as she jerked her hips up and down in the throes of an intense full-body orgasm.

Meanwhile, a *different* kind of grunting noise was coming from Piper's direction, and I turned my head to see the familiar sex flush spreading over her pale skin, but this time her mouth gaped wide open as she trilled her clit rapidly while pressing her other hand harder into her pussy. When she finally let the floodgates open and her body began jerking wildly in the throes of climax, I smiled that she'd finally been able to turn the corner in her journey of sexual self-discovery.

As her fluids gushed out of her pussy, one by one each of the other women began to grunt and howl as they also reached the apex of their pleasure, proudly raising their hips while they squirted their love juices out over their quivering legs and the empty floor in the middle of the circle. No longer able to resist the mounting pressure inside my body, I turned to face Laila who was staring at me intently as her body began shaking and her eyes glazed over in the midst of her own powerful climax. While I watched her beautiful spray jetting out of her pussy onto the floor along with all the other women, I arched my back and growled while I locked eyes with her, coming harder than anytime I'd remembered in my life.

It seemed to take almost a full five minutes from the time the first woman popped off until the last, and when we all finished coming hard while watching each other shaking, moaning, and squirting onto the floor, we collapsed back onto our chairs, staring at the giant puddle of fluid collecting in the middle of the circle.

Venus Spring indeed, I thought, smiling over at Piper whose chest was still bobbing up and down recovering from her first incredible orgasm. *Maybe we should bottle this stuff after all. Judging by the reaction of these women, it certainly seems to be the elixir of feminine power.*

7

—————

That evening, we all enjoyed hamburgers and milkshakes at Danny Meyer's famous Shake Shack in Madison Square Park, laughing and sharing stories about our craziest dates and most unusual sexual encounters. By the time we all drifted back to our hotels close to midnight, we were physically and mentally exhausted. Still, I wondered how many of the women would be able to resist the temptation to try out their newfound ejaculation skills. I had another dream about Laila, this time where she kneeled over my face while pouring her ejaculation juices into my gaping mouth. I had no idea what was in store for our last day together in the workshop, but I was determined to connect with the pretty instructor any way I could.

When we all arrived back at her apartment the following morning, we milled about for a few minutes nibbling on croissants and mini-quiches, then Laila asked us to take our seats. As we peered at each other expectantly, we squirmed in our chairs, barely able to contain our excitement.

"Did you all sleep well last night?" Laila asked.

"Like a baby," Carla said.

"It took a little while to get there," Ava said. "I was on the phone with my husband telling him about what I learned in the workshop, and we both came multiple times while I explained what he could look forward to when I returned."

"Were they nice and juicy orgasms?" Laila smiled.

"Damn right," she said. "I had to replace the towels atop the bed three times!"

"Well, I hope you guys saved a little bit for the grand finale. I thought today we might up the ante a little by *partnering* up this time. Some of you have already expressed your desire to learn how to make your female lovers squirt, and what better forum than a masturbation workshop involving ten women?"

"What if some of us aren't *lesbian*?" Piper said.

"You never know until you try," Laila said. "We're all on the spectrum somewhere. But if you're not comfortable pairing up with another woman, you're welcome to sit aside while you watch the others."

"How do we choose our partners?" Trinity said, glancing over toward Claire, who said she was attracted to women.

"I thought to make it a little more fun, we would assign the pairings by random."

She reached under her chair and pulled out a circular device that looked a bit like a double-layer roulette wheel.

"I've created this counter-rotating Wheel of Fortune spinner that will randomly select each grouping. Are you guys game to give it a try?"

"Okay..." Ava said, shifting nervously in her chair.

Laila brought the device into the middle of the circle and pointed out each of our names placed around the perimeter of the two plates. Then she spun the top plate and the pointer stopped at Carla's name. Everybody hooted and hollered while she stared at the device wondering who she'd be paired with. Laila then spun the bottom plate and it stopped on Ava's name. The group hollered even louder, realizing the two straight women would be paired up as the first couple.

As Laila continued to spin the wheels, one by one each of us got paired with another partner. Trinity got joined with Piper, I was coupled with Claire, Hailey was paired with Molly, which left the last two girls, Penelope and Willow, to join up. As we all looked at our partners excitedly, I peered over at Laila, pinching my eyebrows.

"What about *you*?" I asked. "You're the odd one out. It hardly seems fair that *we'll* be having all the fun."

"Oh, don't worry about me," she smiled. "I'll find a way to keep myself amused while you guys pair up. But if you're offering your services when you're finished with Claire, I'll be happy to join in the festivities."

"Definitely," I said, peering around the group. "We can't leave Laila unattended, can we girls?"

"No way," Trinity said. "Just make sure you save some of your juices for the *rest* of us. I've been keeping my eye on you since the start of the workshop."

"I guess you two will have to arm wrestle to see who goes first," Laila smiled.

"Or *leg* wrestle," Trinity said, winking at me.

"Okay, enough about *me*," Laila said. "This workshop is supposed to be all about you. Go ahead and enjoy yourselves and practice your new squirting skills."

"What if we've never done something like this before?" Piper said. "How do we get started?"

"Sex with a woman isn't so different from having sex with a man. Whether you choose to stimulate each other orally, digitally, or by pressing your bodies together, it's all about exploring your erogenous zones together."

"But if we're hoping to learn how to *squirt* with our partners," Hailey said. "Don't we have to massage our G-Spots while we're stimulating each other? How can we do that if we're rubbing our bodies together?"

"I'm glad you asked, Hailey," Laila smiled, reaching down toward her bag beside her chair. "Because I just happen to have a wide assortment of tools designed for the very thing."

She carried the bag to the center of the circle then one-by-one placed the oddly shaped dildos on a towel on the floor. One was made of clear glass and shaped in the form of an S, with a glass ball on each end. Another one was made of stainless steel and curved in a C-shape with two different-sized bulbs at each end. Yet another was made of silicone and shaped like a curved L with different-shaped protrusions at each end. By the time she'd finished laying out the entire collection, our eyes bulged in shock, wondering how to use them.

"Now you don't have to actually use any of these if you don't want to," Laila said, noticing the look of terror on many of the women's faces. "As we've seen, sometimes the most satisfying way to stimulate the G-spot is with our fingers. There's something to be said for actually *feeling* your partner's physical response as she becomes aroused."

"How exactly do we use some of those things?" Ava said, peering at the S-shaped dildo curiously.

"I'm going to let you guys figure that out for yourself," Laila said. "Each of them is curved in a different way, so you'll just have to experiment with adjusting your body positions until you find one that works for both of you."

"Where do you want us to set up?" Carla said. "It might be hard for both of us to fit on our individual chairs."

"That depends on the manner in which you choose to engage. If you choose to stimulate your partner orally or with your fingers, you might find the curvature of the chairs is ideal for stimulating her clitoris and G-Spot. On the other hand, if you prefer to rub your bodies together, feel free to spread out some towels on the floor and get down and dirty."

Everybody paused for a moment while we peered at Laila, unsure how to proceed.

"Well, what are you waiting for?" Laila said. "We haven't got all day! Remember today's session ends at 2 p.m. to give you enough time to catch your flights back home."

Claire and I peered hesitatingly at one another, then I grabbed her hand, leading her to the side of the living room where I laid each of our towels end-over-end. Trinity was next to approach Piper, crawling up the end of her lounge chair like a prowling cat. Carla picked up one of the double-dildos lying on the floor then kneeled on top of Ava's lap, licking her lips excitedly. By the time each of us had joined up with our appointed partners, I noticed all of the girls melting into each other's arms.

"You don't want to try using one of the *toys*?" Claire said to me as we squatted on the floor.

"Since this is your first time with a woman," I said, I'd rather feel your skin without the help of any sex aid. "There are so many different ways to please a woman."

"So you've done this before?" she said.

"Maybe once or twice," I smiled.

As I leaned in to kiss her, I cupped her breast in my hand, pinching her nipple softly between my fingers. She gasped into my mouth and pressed her mound against the side of my hips. While I watched her chest rising and falling in excitement, I slid my hand down her quivering tummy toward the cleft in her legs, pausing to brush my fingers through her soft muff. It was already sprinkled with dew, and I rubbed her moisture teasingly over her bush like a hairdresser massaging conditioner into her scalp. She spread her legs apart a few inches and raised her hips, eager for me to go lower.

When I rolled my hand over her vulva, I was surprised how wet she already was, and I tickled the inside of her lips by running my fingers up and down the length of her folds, purposefully avoiding her swelling button. Even though I knew she was desperate for me to touch her clit, I was mindful of Laila's earlier instruction to focus on massaging her G-Spot first if I wanted to make her squirt, then move to her clit when she was getting close to orgasm.

When I slipped my two middle fingers into her hole, she shuddered, rolling her tongue around the inside of my mouth, encouraging me to explore further. I pressed my fingers as deep as I could into her cavern, pressing my palm hard against her cunt, and she groaned deeply. Then I curled my fingers slowly upward, pressing them toward the roof of her vagina, feeling the soft tissue near the rear of her canal.

It was fascinating for me to examine another woman's G-Spot clinically for the first time, and as I pulled my fingers closer toward the front of her pussy, I could feel the egg-shaped protrusion swelling and hardening until I reached the horizontal ridges about two joints inside.

Holy smoke, I thought to myself. *It's true that we're all built the same way and every woman is equipped with the same tools to ejaculate.* Up until two days ago, I had no idea that the G-Spot was actually a water-filled bulb surrounding the urethra that we could use to express and squirt at will.

As I continued massaging Claire's bump, her breathing

became more ragged and she began to tighten her body, lifting her hips off the floor. I sensed she was close to coming, and paused for a moment, looking at her pretty face.

"What are you stopping for?" she said, peering at me beseechingly. "I was just about to come!"

"I know," I smiled. "But I want to see you *squirt* when you climax. We're supposed to take it slow, remember? Besides, I want to *taste* you when you come this first time."

Claire's eyes suddenly widened when she realized what I was suggesting, and as I shimmied my body lower down her figure, I peered up at her with a wicked smile.

I'm gonna show this girl how a woman properly gets licked, I thought to myself.

When I positioned my face between her legs, she spread her knees apart and I stared at her vulva for a moment, watching her natural juices dripping down her perineum and over the crack of her ass.

The female prostate isn't the only part of a woman's body that knows how to lubricate the pussy, I smiled.

I lowered my face to her vulva, lapping my tongue against the sides of her slippery lips, then I thrust it inside her hole, curving it up toward her swelling bump.

I have got to do this more often, I thought, feeling the familiar ridges of her G-Spot. *Now that I know how to properly stimulate this organ, this is way too much fun to pass up.*

As I rolled my tongue from side to side over her bulb, Claire mashed her pussy against my face, reveling in her first lesbian experience with oral sex. I could feel her buttocks tightening and her thigh muscles clenching, and knew that she was on the verge of coming once again, and I pulled out, smiling at her as drips of lubrication ran down my chin.

"Oh God, Jade," she pleaded. "I need to come so bad. Don't stop. I want to cum all over your face."

"Okay," I said. "But remember what Laila said. When you feel yourself on the brink of orgasm, don't resist the urge to pee. Remember to bear down and push out at the moment of climax. Give me a warning so I can pull out my fingers and allow you to eject all your fluid."

"Oh, I'll give you a *warning* alright," she panted.

"Okay," I nodded. "I'm going to stimulate you on both sides now. When you're ready, just let it all go."

"I will," Claire nodded excitedly.

When I lowered my face to her pussy, this time I slipped two fingers inside her while I encircled her burning clit between my lips. As I began to bathe her bulb with my undulating tongue, I peered up for a moment to watch the other women around the room. Piper was sitting atop Trinity's face, writhing in ecstasy as the cute African-American girl massaged her G-Spot with her right hand. Hailey and Molly were lying on the floor in a sixty-nine position, eating each other's pussies with their hands buried knuckle-deep in their respective cunts. Ava and Carla had their asses pressed together, rocking their pussies as the curved glass dildo glistening between their flapping vulvas.

Looks like they figured out the right position to use that S-shaped dildo after all, I smiled to myself.

As I peered around the room listening to all the woman groaning and wailing on the verge of orgasm, I suddenly felt Claire's pussy tenting toward the far end, and I peered up at her.

"Yes, Jade," she panted. "I'm going to come now. Fuck, I'm going to cum so hard. I'm going to bathe your beautiful face with my juices."

As she raised her hips higher off the floor and straightened her legs at the edge of climax, I pulled my fingers out of her and watched her perineal muscles pulsing as she squirted her juices all over my blinking face. While she screamed and hollered in orgasmic delight, I smiled with a radiant glow knowing that her first climax with another woman was a full-body experience, where she'd experienced the true pinnacle of pleasure.

As I held her quaking body, letting her juices spray all over my bare tits, I peered around the room, noticing all the other women squirting just as strongly in the full embrace of their partners.

God damn, I thought. *Those Eastern religions had it right. This female ejaculation thing truly is a spiritual experience.*

When the last of the couples had finished ejaculating together, we all lay exhausted in a disheveled heap on the floor, panting and hugging each other happily. But I knew there was still almost two hours left in our workshop and after we all had a quick helping of pizza delivered to the door, we returned to our lounge seats to discuss our experience.

"So, what do you think?" Laila asked with a knowing smile. "Was it as much fun to ejaculate with a partner as it was by self-stimulation?"

"Much more!" Piper interjected, smiling at her partner, Trinity.

"I had no idea having sex with a woman could be as rewarding as with a man," Ava said.

"With the right instruments, *anything* is possible," Laila winked, peering down at their still-glistening glass dildo.

"How about you, Claire?" How did you find your first introduction to girl-on-girl sex?"

"Oh my God," she sighed, peering over at me. "It was even better than I imagined. My only regret is that I won't have even more time in the workshop to spread the love around."

"Something tells me you won't find it so awkward finding new lesbian lovers when you get back home after all this."

Everybody laughed and clapped once again to give recognition for the collective achievement we'd all made in the short time we'd been together.

"We still have a little bit of time left in the workshop," Laila said. "Do you have any questions or would you like to discuss some new techniques for stimulating your partners when you get back home?

"Screw *that*," Trinity said. "We all want to see you get down and dirty now, don't we girls? I'm pretty sure every one of us has been dreaming about fucking you ever since you showed us how to squirt."

"Well, I'm not sure I can accommodate everyone at the same time," Laila smiled. But I might have enough time for one more pairing. How do you want to go about doing this?"

"What about using your magic wheel?" Carla said. "Can you give it one last spin to see which of us gets the chance to make love to you?"

"I suppose that might work," Laila said, lifting the device back onto her lap. "But there's two different wheels with different names on each layer. I'll have to spin it twice to see who wins."

"Go for it," Trinity said, itching at her chance to get together with the sexy instructor.

Laila spun the top plate and when the needle stopped it pointed toward me.

"Woo-hoo!" everybody cheered, peering at me with broad smiles.

"I'm not quite there yet," I said, waiting to see who would be selected when she spun the bottom wheel.

When it finished turning, the needle pointed toward Trinity.

"Hmm," Laila said, feigning dismay. "We seem to have a quandary as to which of you should have your turn."

"Maybe we should have a squirt-off," Trinity joked. "To see who can ejaculate the furthest."

"Or use a bowl to see who can produce the most fluid," I winked.

"Although I'm sure that might be interesting to watch, remember how I said earlier that the best way to ensure a satisfying ejaculation experience is to relax and not feel any pressure to perform? I think we're going to have to find *another* way to decide who I'll pair up with."

Laila removed all the other women's names from the top wheel except mine, then she lifted the name tag for Trinity off the bottom plate and placed it next to mine.

"Are you guys ready?" she said, looking up at the two of us with her hand poised on the needle.

"Are you *kidding* me?" Trinity said. "I'm about to pop off just watching you spinning the wheel! Get on with it. You're killing me here!"

Laila flicked the wheel hard with her finger and all of us watched the needle spinning for a few long moments until it finally stopped against my name.

"Woo-hoo," everybody yelled, eager to get on with the show.

"Sorry, hun," I said, cocking my head toward Trinity. "But someone's gotta do the dirty deed."

"You better make it good, bitch," she smiled back at me.

"Where do you want to do this?" I said, looking at Laila.

"Well, since all of you wanted a piece of me, I suppose it's only fair to do it in the middle of the circle, where everyone can watch."

"Works for me," I said. "Do you have a preference for how we do this? *With* toys or without?"

"Actually, in this case," Laila purred. "I think I'd like to try it *with*. I have a special toy that I like to use for these special occasions."

"Oh?" I said, raising an inquisitive eyebrow.

She reached down into her bag and pulled out a polished wood S-shaped dildo with a carved ball on one end.

"This is called the Noblesse Seduction G-Spot Dildo," Laila said. "It's carved out of real walnut and it has a special place in my heart."

"Not to mention a few *other* special places, I'm sure," I smiled. "I've never used one with that shape before. Is there a special position we need to be in to make it work?"

"There are actually quite a few different positions we could use to enjoy it," she said. "But I had one particular one in mind for you. Why don't you lie down on the floor on your tummy?"

"Um, okay..." I said, happy to assume the submissive position for a change.

As I lay down on the floor with all the other girls perched on the ends of their chairs ready to watch the action, Laila reached into her bag and pulled out a small tube.

"I'm going to lube this up a bit first, to make sure no one gets hurt–"

"I don't think you're going to need much of that," I purred, tilting my glistening pussy up for her to see. "I'm pretty damn wet already just thinking about what you're going to do with that thing."

Laila placed a small dollop of lube on both ends of the gleaming tool, then she kneeled down with her thighs straddling my ass and inserted the thick end in her pussy. Then she twisted the dildo until the curved ball was pointing downward and positioned it against my flaring lips.

"Uhnnn," I groaned, feeling it rubbing against my opening. "I like the feel of that. It's nice and smooth."

"And *hard*," Laila said, pressing her hips forward and inserting the device into my pussy.

I could feel the curved ball pressing down against the roof of my vagina, and as she began to rock her hips toward my ass, it slid over my bulging G-Spot, stimulating me unlike any dildo I'd felt before.

"Fuck yes," I purred. "Fuck me with your pretty brown dildo, Laila. Massage my G-Spot with your big curved dick. I like it when you fuck me from behind."

"Yeah?" Laila said, taunting me. "Do you like it as much as a man's cock? Do you like it this hard?"

"It's harder than any *man* I've known, that's for sure," I purred. "But knowing it's attached to a pretty girl makes it a lot more exciting for me."

"You like getting fucked by girls?"

"Sometimes," I grunted as she slapped her mound harder against my ass. This was the first time during the workshop where I'd heard her talk dirty, and it was turning me on like crazy. "Especially one who knows what she's doing."

"Are you ready to come with me?" she panted, rocking her hips more forcefully against my ass.

"God, yes," I growled.

I could feel my G-Spot swelling as she continued massaging it with the flared bulb of the dildo, and as I began to feel shoots of electricity running up and down my thighs,

I reached behind me, digging my nails into the side of her hips, pulling her harder toward me.

"I'm going to squirt all over your pretty pussy when I come," I groaned. "I almost there. Oh *fuckkkk...*"

Suddenly, Laila pulled out of me and tossed the wooden dildo to the side as we both howled at the top of our lungs, spraying our juices all over each other while the rest of the girls gaped at us with wide eyes. As Laila started spraying over my quivering ass, I tilted my hips up toward her, squirting my juices against her flapping cunt like a firehose. When we finally collapsed onto one another in a giant puddle of clear fluid on the floor, the entire room erupted in an enormous round of applause.

Talk about a 'hands-on' workshop, I smiled to myself, panting heavily beside Laila. *This Fountain of Venus seminar has taken the concept to an entirely new level.*

R*eady for more erotic chills and thrills? Order the next exciting volume in Jade's Erotic Adventures:*

Sometimes you just wanna watch...

ALSO BY VICTORIA RUSH

Wet your whistle a hundred different ways with Jade's Erotic Adventures. Browse the full collection of Victoria Rush steamy stories here:

Click to scan your favorites...

FOLLOW VICTORIA RUSH:

Want to keep informed of my latest erotic book releases? Sign up for my newsletter and receive a FREE bonus book:

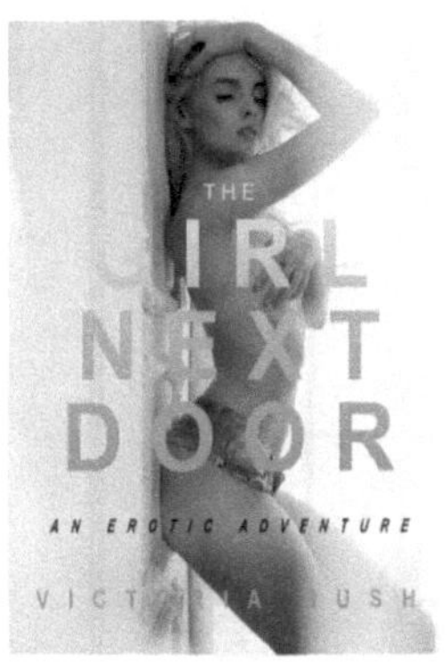

Spying on the neighbors just got a lot more interesting...